D0343841

For the baby

VIKING KESTREL

Penguin Books Ltd, Harmondsworth, Middlesex, England
Viking Penguin Inc., 40 West 23rd Street, New York, New York 10010, U.S.A.
Penguin Books Australia Ltd, Ringwood, Victoria, Australia
Penguin Books Canada Ltd, 2801 John Street, Markham, Ontario, Canada L3R 1B4
Penguin Books (N.Z.) Ltd, 182–190 Wairau Road, Auckland 10, New Zealand

First published 1981
Reprinted 1982, 1983, and 1986

Copyright © Janet and Allan Ahlberg, 1981

All rights reserved. Without limiting the rights under copyright
reserved above, no part of this publication may be reproduced,
stored in or introduced into a retrieval system, or transmitted,
in any form or by any means (electronic, mechanical, photocopying,
recording or otherwise), without the prior written permission
of both the copyright owner and the above publisher of this book.

ISBN 0–670–80344–8

Printed in Hong Kong

PEEPO!

by

Janet & Allan Ahlberg

VIKING KESTREL

Here's a little baby
One, two, three
Stands in his cot
What does he see?

PEEPO!

He sees his father sleeping
  In the big brass bed
And his mother too
  With a hairnet on her head.

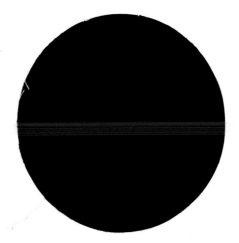

He sees the shadows moving
  On the bedroom wall
And the sun at the window
  And his teddy
  And his ball.

Here's a little baby
One, two, three
Sits in his high chair
What does he see?

PEEPO!

He sees his mother pouring
  Hot porridge in a bowl
And his father in the doorway
  With a bucketful of coal.

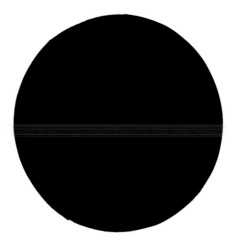

He sees his sisters skipping
  In the yard outside
And his grandma pegging washing
  On the clothes-line
  To be dried.

Here's a little baby
One, two, three
Sits in his pushchair
What does he see?

PEEPO!

He sees a bonfire smoking
  Pigeons in the sky
His mother cleaning windows
  A dog going by.

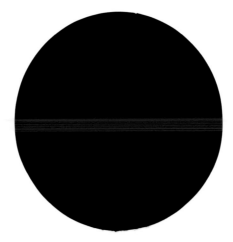

He sees his sisters searching
  For a jar or tin
To take up to the park
  And catch fishes in.

Here's a little baby
One, two, three
Sits on the grass
What does he see?

PEEPO!

He sees his sisters fishing
  With a brown stocking net
And dresses tucked in knickers
  And legs shiny wet.

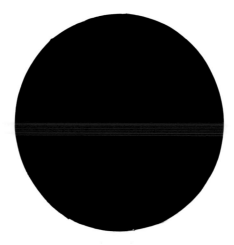

He sees the tassels blowing
  On his grandma's shawl
And the fringe on the pushchair
  And his teddy
  And his ball.

Here's a little baby
One, two, three
Sits on his sister's lap
What does he see?

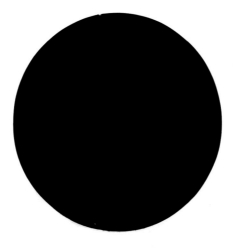

PEEPO!

He sees his grandma ironing
His father pouring tea
His other sister squabbling
She wants him on *her* knee.

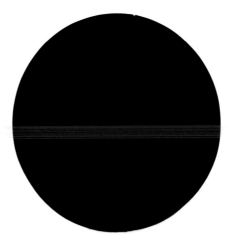

He sees his mother dozing
In the easy chair
And a dog in the doorway
Who shouldn't be there.

Here's a little baby
One, two, three
Sits in his bath-tub
What does he see?

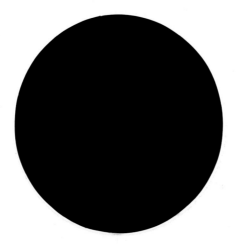

PEEPO!

He sees his father kneeling
  With his sleeves rolled up
And the flannel on the table
  And the soap
  In a cup.

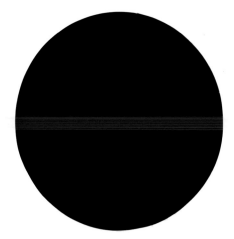

He sees his nightie warming
  On the oven door
His sisters in the clothes-horse
  Puddles on the floor.

Here's a little baby
One, two, three
On his way to bed
What does he see?

PEEPO!

He sees the landing mirror
  With its rainbow rim
And a mother with a baby
  Just like him.

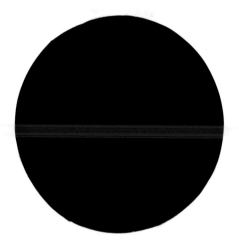

He sees the bedroom door
  The cot made ready
His father kissing him goodnight
  His ball
  And his teddy.

Here's a little baby
One, two, three
Fast asleep and dreaming
What did he see?

THE END